This book is dedicated to
Hannah's sister Isabelle, brother Jordan,
and her best friend Alexa.

If you ever
make it down to the
Old Town Safari.

There is something that
you will need to see!

For in this safari
lives a lonely giraffe.
All the others just
look at him and laugh.

For this giraffe has peculiar taste.
He doesn't eat like the others
and doesn't waste.

He only eats pizza which is quite funny to see.

Although he'll only eat cheese, no pepperoni.

It all started when he was a young age of three. His mother called him Monnie, and only ate from the big tree.

One day a little girl came
to see her favorite herbivore.

She was given a chance
to feed them by
joining a safari tour.

She held lettuce in one hand and her pizza in the other.
Her nerves were high, so she stayed close to her mother.

There stood a tall giraffe, and her baby looking scared right behind.
As the girl approached and said, don't worry I'll be kind.

She extended her hand to feed the
little guy and moved closer and closer.

To her surprise, his tongue came
out and grabbed the pizza from her.

Several days later, Monnie's
mother noticed he
just wouldn't eat.
He was just so hungry
he couldn't even stand on his feet.

The girl approached once again with a whole pizza in her hand.

Monnie's hunger soon disappeared like hourglass sand.

Over the years, his keepers realized
the only food he would eat.
So for every meal from that day forward
pizza would be his treat.

The others didn't talk to him because they thought he was odd.

They pointed and laughed at him and never let him in their pod.

Then one day Monnie approached the others and placed pizza at their feet.

He said, give it a try and you will see it will make you feel complete.

When the others decided to give it a try, Monnie trembled in fear.

He was not sure if they would love it the way he did year after year.

The others ate the pizza, with huge smiles
now feeling quite upbeat.
They said we were wrong to judge you
Monnie, It's delicious and now
it's all we'll eat.

There is a lesson to be learned here that we should always hold as true. Don't judge others if they have different likes than you.

Now if you ever make it to the
Old Town Safari, don't forget to bring.
Pizza for Monnie and his
friends, which will make
them sing:

"Old Town Safari is our home and Pizza is all we eat!"

THE END

The main character of this story is based on a stuffed animal that was given to Hannah from the Bronx zoo when she was 2. Right away she named him Monnie and he quickly became her favorite stuffed animal. Years later, she had a chance to feed giraffes and the idea for this book was created. Hannah and her dad had a blast working on this story and we hope you have as much fun reading it as much as we had writing it.